UNHAPPY FAR–OFF THINGS

UNHAPPY
FAR-OFF THINGS

BY
LORD DUNSANY

Published by
Wildside Press, LLC
P.O. Box 301
Holicong, PA 18928-0301 USA
www.wildsidepress.com

Wildside Press Edition: MMIII

A Dirge of Victory

Lift not thy trumpet, Victory, to the sky
  Nor through battalions nor by batteries blow
  But over hollows full of old wire go
Where among dregs of war the long-dead lie
With wasted iron that the guns passed by
  When they went eastwards like a tide at flow
  There blow thy trumpet that the dead may
    know,
Who waited for thy coming, Victory.

It is not we that have deserved thy wreath.
  They waited there among the towering weeds :
The deep mud burned under the thermite's
    breath,
  And winter cracked the bones that no man
    heeds :
Hundreds of nights flamed by : the seasons
    passed,
And thou hast come to them at last, at last !

FOREWORD

I HAVE chosen a title that shall show
that I make no claim for this book to be
"up-to-date." As the first tale indicates
I hoped to show, to as many as might care
to read my words, something of the extent
of the wrongs that the people of France
had suffered. There is no such need any
longer. The tales, so far as they went, I
gather together here for those that read
my books.

CONTENTS

THE CATHEDRAL OF ARRAS

I

THE CATHEDRAL OF ARRAS

ON the great steps of Arras Cathedral
I saw a procession, in silence, standing still.

They were in orderly and perfect lines,
stirring or swaying slightly. Sometimes
they bent their heads, sometimes two leaned
together, but for the most part they were
motionless. It was the time when the
fashion was just changing and some were
newly all in shining yellow, while others
still wore green.

I went up the steps amongst them, the
only human thing, for men and women
worship no more in Arras Cathedral, and
the trees have come instead; little humble
things all less than four years old, in great
numbers thronging the steps processionally,
and growing in perfect rows just where

step meets step. They have come to Arras
with the wind and the rain; which enter the
aisles together whenever they will, and go
wherever man went; they have such a
reverent air, the young limes on the three
flights of steps, that you would say they
did not know that Arras Cathedral was
fallen on evil days, that they did not know
they looked on ruin and vast disaster, but
thought that these great walls open to stars
and sun were the natural and fitting place
for the worship of little weeds.

Behind them the shattered houses of
Arras seemed to cluster about the cathedral
as, one might fancy easily, hurt and fright-
ened children, so wistful are their gaping
windows and old, gray, empty gables, so
melancholy and puzzled. They are more
like a little old people come upon trouble,
gazing at their great elder companion and
not knowing what to do.

But the facts of Arras are sadder than a
poet's most tragic fancies. In the western
front of Arras Cathedral stand eight pillars

rising from the ground; above them stood four more. Of the four upper pillars the two on the left are gone, swept away by shells from the North: and a shell has passed through the neck of one of the two that is left just as a bullet might go through a daffodil's stem.

The left-hand corner of that western wall has been caught from the North, by some tremendous shell which has torn the whole corner down in a mound of stone: and still the walls have stood.

I went in through the western doorway. All along the nave lay a long heap of white stones, with grass and weeds on the top, and a little trodden path over the grass and weeds. This is all that remained of the roof of Arras Cathedral and of any chairs or pews there may have been in the nave, or anything that may have hung above them. It was all down but one slender arch that crossed the nave just at the transept; it stood out against the sky, and all who saw it wondered how it stood.

In the southern aisle panes of green glass, in twisted frames of lead, here and there lingered, like lonely leaves on an apple-tree after a hailstorm in spring. The aisles still had their roofs over them which those stout old walls held up in spite of all.

Where the nave joins the transept the ruin is most enormous. Perhaps there was more to bring down there, so the Germans brought it down: there may have been a tower there, for all I know, or a spire.

I stood on the heap and looked towards the altar. To my left all was ruin. To my right two old saints in stone stood by the southern door. The door had been forced open long ago, and stood as it was opened, partly broken. A great round hole gaped in the ground outside; it was this that had opened the door.

Just beyond the big heap, on the left of the chancel, stood something made of wood, which almost certainly had been the organ.

As I looked at these things there passed through the desolate sanctuaries, and down

an aisle past pillars pitted with shrapnel,
a sad old woman, sad even for a woman of
Northeast France. She seemed to be
looking after the mounds and stones that
had once been the Cathedral; perhaps she
had once been the Bishop's servant, or the
wife of one of the vergers; she only remained of all who had been there in other
days, she and the pigeons and jackdaws.
I spoke to her. All Arras, she said, was
ruined. The great Cathedral was ruined;
her own family were ruined utterly, and
she pointed to where the sad houses gazed
from forlorn dead windows. Absolute ruin,
she said; but there must be no armistice.
No armistice. No. It was necessary that
there should be no armistice at all. No
armistice with Germans.

She passed on, resolute and sad, and the
guns boomed on beyond Arras.

A French interpreter, with the Sphinxes'
heads on his collar, showed me a picture
postcard with a photograph of the chancel
as it was five years ago. It was the very

chancel before which I was standing. To
see that photograph astonished me, and to
know that the camera that took it must
have stood where I was standing, only a
little lower down, under the great heap.

Though one knew there had been an
altar there, and candles and roof and carpet,
and all the solemnity of a cathedral's in-
terior, yet to see that photograph and to
stand on that weedy heap, in the wind,
under the jackdaws, was a contrast with
which the mind fumbled.

I walked a little with the French interpreter. We came to a little shrine in the
southern aisle. It had been all paved
with marble, and the marble was broken
into hundreds of pieces, and some one had
carefully picked up all the bits, and laid
them together on the altar.

And this pathetic heap that was gathered
of broken bits had drawn many to stop and
gaze at it; and idly, as soldiers will, they
had written their names on them: every
bit had a name on it. With but a touch of

irony the Frenchman said "All that is
necessary to bring your name to posterity
is to write it on one of these stones." "No,"
I said, "I will do it by describing all this."
And we both laughed.

I have not done it yet: there is more to
say of Arras. As I begin the tale of ruin
and wrong, the man who did it totters.
His gaudy power begins to stream away
like the leaves of autumn. Soon his throne
will be bare, and I shall have but begun to
say what I have to say of calamity in
cathedral and little gardens of Arras.

The winter of the Hohenzollerns will
come; sceptre, uniforms, stars and courtiers
all gone; still the world will not know half
of the bitter wrongs of Arras. And spring
will bring a new time and cover the trenches
with green, and the pigeons will preen
themselves on the shattered towers, and
the lime trees along the steps will grow
taller and brighter, and happier men will
sing in the streets untroubled by any War
Lord; by then perhaps I may have told, to

such as care to read, what such a war did
in an ancient town, already romantic when
romance was young, when war came suddenly without mercy, without pity, out of
the North and East, on little houses, carved
galleries and gardens; churches, cathedrals
and the jackdaw nests.

A GOOD WAR

II

A GOOD WAR

NIETZSCHE said: "You have heard that a good cause justifies any war, but I say unto you that a good war justifies any cause."

A man was walking alone over a plain so desolate that, if you have never seen it, the mere word desolation could never convey to you the melancholy surroundings that mourned about this man on his lonely walk. Far off a vista of trees followed a cheerless road all dead as mourners suddenly stricken dead in some funeral procession. By this road he had come; but when he had reached a certain point he turned from the road at once, branching away to the left, led by a line of bushes that may once have been a lane. For some while his feet had rustled

through long-neglected grass; ' sometimes
he lifted them up to step over a telephone
wire that lolled over old entanglements and
bushes; often he came to rusty strands of
barbed wire and walked through them where
they had been cut, perhaps years ago, by
huge shells; then his feet hissed on through
the grass again, dead grass that had hissed
about his boots all through the afternoon.

Once he sat down to rest on the edge of a
crater, weary with such walking as he had
never seen before; and after he had stayed
there a little while a cat that seemed to have
its home in that wild place started suddenly
up and leaped away over the weeds. It
seemed an animal totally wild, and utterly
afraid of man.

Grey bare hills surrounded the waste: a
partridge called far off: evening was draw-
ing in. He rose wearily, and yet with a
certain fervour, as one that pursues with
devotion a lamentable quest. Looking
round him as he left his resting place he
saw a cabbage or two that after some while

had come back to what was a field and had
sprouted on the edge of a shell-hole. A
yellowing convolvulus climbed up a dead
weed. Weeds, grass and tumbled earth
were all about him. It would be no better
when he went on. Still he went on. A
flower or two peeped up among the weeds.
He stood up and looked at the landscape
and drew no hope from that; the shattered
trunk of a stricken tree leered near him,
white trenches scarred the hill side.

He followed an old trench through a
hedge of elder, passed under more wire, by
a great rusty shell that had not burst,
passed by a dug-out where something grey
seemed to lie down at the bottom of many
steps. Black fungi grew near the entrance.
He went on and on over shell-holes, passing
round them where they were deep, stepping
into or over the small ones. Little burrs
clutched at him; he went rustling on, the
only sound in the waste but the clicking of
shattered iron. Now he was among nettles.
He came by many small unnatural valleys.

He passed more trenches only guarded by fungi.

While it was light he followed little paths, marvelling who made them. Once he got into a trench. Dandelions leaned across it as though to bar his way, believing man to have gone and to have no right to return. Weeds thronged in thousands here. It was the day of the weeds. It was only they that seemed to triumph in those fields deserted of man. He passed on down the trench, and never knew whose trench it once had been. Frightful shells had smashed it here and there, and had twisted iron as though round gigantic fingers, that had twiddled it idly a moment and let it drop to lie in the rain for ever.

He passed more dug-outs and black fungi watching them, and then he left the trench, going straight on over the open: again dead grasses hissed about his feet, sometimes small wire sang faintly. He passed through a belt of nettles and thence to dead grass again. And now the light of the afternoon was beginning to dwindle away. He had intended to reach his journey's end by daylight, for he was past the time of life when one wanders after dark, but he had not contemplated the difficulty of walking over that road or dreamed that lanes he knew should be so foundered and merged in that mournful desolate moor.

Evening was falling fast, still he kept on. It was the time when the cornstacks would once have begun to grow indistinct and slowly turn grey in the greyness, and homesteads one by one would have lit their innumerable lights. But evening now came down on a dreary desolation: and a cold wind arose; and the traveller heard the mournful sound of iron flapping on broken things, and knew that this was the sound that would haunt the waste for ever.

And evening settled down, a huge grey canvas waiting for sombre pictures, a setting for all the dark tales of the world, haunted if ever a grizzly place was haunted ever in any century, in any land; but not

by mere ghosts from all those thousands
of graves and half-buried bodies and sepul-
chral shell-holes; haunted by things huger
and more disastrous than that; haunted
by wailing ambitions, under the stars or
moon, drifting across the rubbish that once
was villages, which strews the lonely plain;
the lost ambitions of two Emperors and a
Sultan, wailing from wind to wind, and
whimpering for dominion of the world.

The cold wind blew over the blasted
heath and bits of broken iron flapped on
and on.

And now the traveller hurried, for night
was falling, and such a night as three witches
might have brewed in a cauldron. He
went on eagerly but with infinite sadness.
Over the sky line strange rockets went up
from the war, peered oddly over the earth
and went down again. Very far off a few
soldiers lit a little fire of their own. The
night grew colder; tap, tap went broken
iron.

And at last the traveller stopped in the

lonely night, and looked round him attentively, and appeared to be satisfied that he
had come within sight of his journey's end,
although to ordinary eyes the spot to which
he had come differed in no way from the
rest of the waste.

He went no further but turned round
and round, peering piece by piece at that
weedy and cratered earth.

He was looking for the village where he
was born.

THE HOUSE WITH TWO STORIES

III

THE HOUSE WITH TWO STORIES

I CAME again to Croisilles.

I looked for the sunken road that we used to hold in support, with its row of little shelters in the bank and the carved oak saints above them here and there that had survived the church in Croisilles. I could have found it with my eyes shut. With my eyes open I could not find it. I did not recognise the lonely metalled road down which lorries were rushing for the little lane so full of life, whose wheel-ruts were three years old.

As I gazed about me looking for our line I passed an old French civilian looking down at a slight mound of white stone that rose a little higher than the road. He was walking about uncertainly, when first I noticed him, as though he was not sure where he was. But now he stood quite still, looking down at the mound.

"*Voilà ma maison*," he said.

He said no more than that: this astounding remark, this gesture that indicated such calamity, were quite simply made. There was nothing whatever of theatrical pose that we wrongly associate with the French because they conceal their emotions less secretly than we; there were no tragic tones in his voice: only a trace of deep affection showed in one of the words he used. He spoke as a woman might say of her only child, "Look at *my* baby."

"*Voilà ma maison*," he said.

I tried to say in his language what I felt; and after my attempt he spoke of his house.

It was very old. Down underneath, he said, it dated from feudal times; though I did not quite make out whether all that lay under that mound had been so old or whether he only meant the cellars of his house. It was a fine high house, he said; as much as two stories high. No one that is familiar with houses of fifty stories, none even that has known palaces, will smile at this old man's efforts to tell of his high house, and to make me believe that it rose to two stories high, as we stood together by that sad white mound. He told me his son was killed. And that disaster strangely did not move me so much as the white mound that had been a house and had had two stories, for it seems to be common to every French family with whose fathers I have chanced to speak in ruined cities or on busy roads of France.

He pointed to a huge white mound beyond on the top of which some one had stuck a small cross of wood. "The church," he said. And that I knew already.

In very inadequate French I tried to comfort him. I told him that surely France would build his house again. Perhaps even the Allies; for I could not believe that we shall have done enough if we merely drive the Germans out of France and leave this poor old man still wandering homeless. I told him that surely in the future Croisilles would stand again.

He took no interest in anything that I said. His house of two stories was down, his son was dead, the little village of Croisilles had gone away; he had only one hope from the future. When I had finished speaking of the future, he raised a knobbed thick stick that he carried, up to the level of his throat, surely his son's old trench stick, and there he let it dangle from a piece of string in the handle, which he held against his neck. He watched me shrewdly and attentively meanwhile, for I was a stranger and was to be taught something I might not know, a thing that was necessary for all men to learn. "*Le Kaiser*," he said. "Yes," I said, "the Kaiser." But I pronounced the word Kaiser differently from him, and he repeated again "*Le Kaiser*", and watched me closely to be sure that I understood. And then he

said "*Pendu*", and made the stick quiver a
little as it dangled from its string. "*Oui*,"
I said, "*Pendu.*"

Did I understand? He was not yet
quite sure. It was important that this
thing should be quite decided between us
as we stood on this road through what had
been Croisilles, where he had lived through
many sunny years and I had dwelt for a
season amongst rats. "*Pendu! Pendu!*"
he said. Yes, I agreed.

It was all right. The old man almost
smiled.

I offered him a cigarette and we lit two
from an apparatus of flint and steel and
petrol that the old man had in his pocket.

He showed me a photograph of himself
and a passport to prove, I suppose, that he
was not a spy. One could not recognise
the likeness, for it must have been taken
on some happier day, before he had seen
his house of two stories lying there by the
road. But he was no spy, for there were
tears in his eyes; and Prussians, I think,

have no tears for what we saw as we gazed across the village of Croisilles.

I spoke of the rebuilding of his house no more, I spoke no more of the new Croisilles shining through the future years; for these were not the things that he saw in the future and these were not the hopes of the poor old man. He had one dark hope of the future, and no others. He hoped to see the Kaiser hung for the wrong he had done to Croisilles. It was for this hope he lived.

Madame or Señor of whatever far country, who may chance to see these words, blame not this old man for the fierce hope he cherished. It was the only hope he had. You, Madame, with your garden, your house, your church, the village where all know you, you may hope as a Christian should; there is wide room for hope in your future. You shall see the seasons move over your garden, you shall busy yourself with your home, and speak and share with your neighbors innumerable small joys, and find consolation and beauty, and at last rest, in and around the church whose spire you see from your home. You, Señor, with your son perhaps growing up, perhaps wearing already some sword that you wore once, you can turn back to your memories, or look with hope to the future, with equal ease.

The man that I met in Croisilles had none of these things at all. He had that one hope only.

Do not, I pray you, by your voice or vote, or by any power or influence that you have, do anything to take away from this poor old Frenchman the only little hope that he has left. The more trivial his odd hope appears to you compared with your own high hopes that come so easily to you amongst all your fields and houses, the more cruel a thing must it be to take it from him.

I learned many things in Croisilles, and the last of them is this strange one the old man taught me. I turned and shook hands with him and said Good-bye, for I wished to see again our old front line that we used to hold over the hill, now empty, silent at last. "The Boche is defeated," I said. "*Vaincu, Vaincu*," he repeated. And I left him with something almost like happiness looking out of his tearful eyes.

BERMONDSEY VERSUS WURTEMBURG

IV

BERMONDSEY VERSUS WURTEMBURG

THE trees grew thinner and thinner along the road, then ceased altogether, and suddenly we saw Albert in the wood of the ghosts of murdered trees, all grey and deserted.

Descending into Albert past trees in their agony we came all at once on the houses. You did not see them far off as in other cities; we came on them all at once as you come on a corpse in the grass.

We stopped and stood by a house that was covered with plaster marked off to look like great stones, its pitiful pretence laid bare, the slates gone and the rooms gone, the plaster all pitted with shrapnel. Near it lay an iron railing, a handrail

blown there from the railway bridge; a
shrapnel bullet had passed through its
twisted stem as though it had gone through
butter. And beside the handrail lay one
of the great steel supports of the bridge,
that had floated there upon some flaming
draught; the end of it bent and splayed
as though it had been a slender cane that
some one had shoved too hard into the earth.

There had been a force abroad in Albert
that could do these things, an iron force
that had no mercy for iron, a mighty
mechanical contrivance that could take
machinery and pull it all to pieces in a
moment as a child takes a flower to pieces
petal by petal.

When such a force was abroad what
chance had man? It had come down upon
Albert suddenly, and railway lines and
bridges had dropped and withered, and
the houses had stooped down in the blasting
heat, and in that attitude I found them
still, — worn-out, melancholy heaps over-
come by disaster.

Pieces of paper rustled about like footsteps, dirt covered the ruins, fragments of
rusty shells lay as unsightly and dirty as
that which they had destroyed. Cleaned
up and polished, and priced at half-a-
crown apiece, these fragments may look
romantic some day in a London shop;
but to-day in Albert they look unclean and
untidy like a cheap knife sticking up from
a murdered woman's ribs, whose dress is
long out of fashion.

The stale smell of war arose from the
desolation.

A British helmet dented in like an old
bowler, but tragic, not absurd, lay near
a barrel and a teapot.

On a wall that rose above a heap of dirty
and smashed rafters was written in red
paint KOMP⁰ I. M. B. K. 184. The red
paint had dripped down the wall from
every letter. Verily we stood upon the
scene of the murder.

Opposite those red letters across the road
was a house with traces of a pleasant

ornament below the sills of the windows, a design of grapes and vine. Some one had stuck up a wooden boot on a peg outside the door.

Perhaps the cheery design on the wall attracted me. I entered the house and looked round.

A chunk of shell lay on the floor, and a little decanter, only chipped at the lip, and part of a haversack of horse-skin. There were pretty tiles on the floor, but dry mud buried them deep: it was like the age-old dirt that gathers in temples in Africa. A man's waistcoat lay on the mud and part of a woman's stays: the waistcoat was black and was probably kept for Sundays. That was all that there was to see on the ground floor; no more flotsam than that had come down to these days from peace.

A forlorn stairway tried still to wind upstairs. It went up out of a corner of the room. It seemed still to believe that there was an upper story, still to feel that this

was a house; there seemed a hope in the
twists of that battered staircase that men
would yet come again and seek sleep at
evening by the way of those broken steps;
the handrail and the banisters streamed
down from the top, a woman's dress lolled
down from the upper room above those
aimless steps, the laths of the ceiling
gaped, the plaster was gone; of all the hopes
men hope that can never be fulfilled, of
all desires that ever come too late, most
futile was the hope expressed by that stairway's posture that ever a family would
come home there again or tread those
steps once more. And, if in some far
country one should hope, who has not seen
Albert, out of compassion for these poor
people of France, that where a staircase still
remains there may be enough of a house to
shelter those who called it home again, I
will tell one thing more: there blew inside
that house the same wind that blew outside,
the wind that wandered free over miles of
plains wandered unchecked through that

house; there was no indoors or outdoors any more.

And on the wall of the room in which I stood, some one had proudly written his regiment's name, The 156th Wurtemburgers. It was written in chalk; and another man had come and had written two words before it and had recorded the name of his own regiment too. And the writing that remains after these two men are gone, and the lonely house is silent but for the wind and the things that creak as it blows, the only message of this deserted house, is this mighty record, this rare line of history, illwritten: "Lost by the 156th Wurtemburgers, retaken by the Bermondsey Butterflies."

Two men wrote that sentence between them. And, as with Homer, no one knows who they were. And like Homer their words were epic.

ON AN OLD BATTLE FIELD

V

ON AN OLD BATTLE FIELD

I ENTERED an old battle field through a garden gate, a pale green gate by the Bapaume-Arras road. The cheerful green attracted me in the deeps of the desolation as an emerald might in a dust-bin. I entered through that homely garden gate: it had no hinges, no pillars, it lolled on a heap of stone. I came to it from the road; this alone was not battle field; the road alone was made and tended and kept; all the rest was battle field as far as the eye could see. Over a large whitish heap lay a Virginia creeper, turning a dull crimson. And the presence of this creeper mourning there in the waste showed unmistakably that the heap had been a house. All the living things were gone that had called this white heap Home: the father would be fighting somewhere; the children would have fled, if there had been time; the dog would have gone with them, or perhaps, if there was not time, he served other masters; the cat would have made a lair for herself and stalked mice at night through the trenches. All the live things that we ever consider were gone; the creeper alone remained, the only mourner, clinging to fallen stones that had supported it once.

And I knew by its presence here there had been a house. And by the texture or composition of the ruin all round I saw that a village had stood there. There are calamities one does not contemplate, when one thinks of time and change. Death, passing away, even ruin, are all the human lot; but one contemplates ruin as brought by kindly ages, coming slowly at last, with lichen and ivy and moss, its harsher aspects all hidden with green, coming with dignity and in due season. Thus our works should pass away; our worst fears contemplated no more than this.

But, here in a single day, perhaps in a
moment with one discharge from a battery,
all the little things that one family cared
for, their house, their garden, and the
garden paths, and then the village and the
road through the village, and the old land-
marks that the old people remembered, and
countless treasured things, were all turned
into rubbish.

And these things that one did not contemplate have happened for hundreds of miles,
with such disaster vast plains and hills are
covered, because of the German war.

Deep wells, old cellars, battered trenches
and dug-outs, lie in the rubbish and weeds
under the intricate wreckage of peace and
war. It will be a bad place years hence
for wanderers lost at night.

When the village went, trenches came;
and, in the same storm that had crumbled
the village, the trenches withered too;
shells still thump on to the North, but
peace and war alike have deserted the village. Grass has begun to return over torn

earth on edges of trenches.   Abundant wire
rusts away by its twisted stakes of steel.
Not a path of old, not a lane nor a doorway
there, but is barred and cut off by wire;
and the wire in its turn has been cut by
shells and lies in ungathered swathes.   A
pair of wheels moulders amongst weeds,
and may be of peace or of war, it is too
broken down for any one to say.   A great
bar of iron lies cracked across as though one
of the elder giants had handled it carelessly.
Another mound near by with an old green
beam sticking out of it was also once a
house.   A trench runs by it.   A German
bomb with its wooden handle, some bottles,
a bucket, a petrol tin and some bricks and
stones, lie in the trench.   A young elder
tree grows amongst them.   And over all
the ruin and rubbish Nature with all her
wealth and luxury comes back to her old
inheritance, holding again the land that
she held so long, before the houses came.

A garden gate of iron has been flung
across a well.   Then a deep cellar into

which a whole house seems to have slanted
down. In the midst of all this is an orchard. A huge shell has uprooted, but not
killed, an apple-tree; another apple-tree
stands stone dead on the edge of a crater:
most of the trees are dead.

British aeroplanes drone over continually.
A great gun goes by towards Bapaume,
dragged by a slow engine with caterpillar
wheels. The gun is all blotched green and
yellow. Four or five men are seated on
the huge barrel alone.

Dark old steps near the orchard run
down into a dug-out, with a cartridge-case
tied to a piece of wood beside it to beat
when the gas came. A telephone wire lies
listlessly by the opening. A patch of
Michaelmas daisies, deep mauve and pale
mauve, and a bright yellow flower beside
them, show where a garden used to stand
near by. Above the dug-out a patch of
jagged earth shows in three clear layers
under the weeds: four inches of grey road-
metal, imported, for all this country is chalk

and clay; two inches of flint below it; and under that an inch of a bright red stone. We are looking then at a road, a road through a village trodden by men and women, and the hooves of horses and familiar modern things, a road so buried, so shattered, so overgrown, showing by chance an edge in the midst of the wilderness, that I could seem rather to have discovered the track of the Dinosaur in prehistoric clays than the highway of a little village that only five years ago was full of human faults and joys and songs and tiny tears. Down that road before the plans of the Kaiser began to fumble with the earth, down that road, — but it is useless to look back, we are too far away from five years ago, too far away from thousands of ordinary things, that never seemed as though they would ever peer at us over chasms of time, out of another age, utterly far off, irrevocably removed from our ways and days. They are gone, those times, gone like the Dinosaur, gone with bows and arrows and the old knightlier days. No splendour marks their sunset where I sit, no dignity of ruined houses, or derelict engines of war; all equally are scattered dirtily in the mud, and common weeds overpower them; it is not ruin but rubbish that covers the ground here and spreads its untidy flood for hundreds and hundreds of miles.

A band plays in Arras, to the North and East the shells go thumping on.

The very origins of things are in doubt, so much is jumbled together. It is as hard to make out just where the trenches ran, and which was No Man's Land, as it is to tell the houses from garden and orchard and road: the rubbish covers all. It is as though the ancient forces of Chaos had come back from the abyss to fight against order and man, and Chaos had won. So lies this village of France.

As I left it a rat, with something in its mouth, holding its head high, ran right across the village.

THE REAL THING

VI

THE REAL THING

ONCE at manoeuvres, as the Prussian Crown Prince charged at the head of his regiment; as sabres gleamed, plumes streamed, and hooves thundered behind him, he is reported to have said to one that galloped near him: "Ah! If only this were the real thing!"

One need not doubt that the report is true. So a young man might feel as he led his regiment of cavalry, for the scene would fire the blood; all those young men and fine uniforms and good horses, all coming on behind, everything streaming that could float on the air, everything jingling then which could ever make a sound, a bright sky no doubt over the uniforms, a good fresh wind for men and horses to gulp; and, behind, the clinking and jingling, the long roll of hooves thundering. Such a scene might well stir emotions to sigh for the splendours of battle.

This is one side of war. Mutilation and death are another; misery, cold and dirt; pain, and the intense loneliness of men left behind by armies, with much to think of, no hope, and a day or two to live. But we understand that glory covers that.

There is yet a third side.

I came to Albert when the fight was far from it; only at night you saw any signs of war, when clouds flashed now and then and curious rockets peered. Albert robbed of peace was deserted even by war.

I will not say that Albert was devastated or desolate, for these long words have different interpretations and may easily be exaggerated. A German agent might say to you "Devastated is rather a strong word, and desolate is a matter of opinion."

And so you might never know what Albert is like.

I will tell you what I saw.

Albert was a large town. I will not write of all of it.

I sat down near a railway bridge at the edge of the town; I think I was near the station; and small houses had stood there with little gardens; such as porters and other railway folk would have lived in. I sat down on the railway and looked at one of these houses, for it had clearly been a house. It was at the back of it that most remained, in what must have been a garden. A girder torn up like a pack of cards lay on the leg of a table amongst a brick wall by an apple-tree.

Lower down in the heap was the framework of a large four-poster bed; through it all a vine came up quite green and still alive; and at the edge of the heap lay a doll's green pram. Small though the house had been there was evidence in that heap of some prosperity in more than one

generation. For the four-poster bed had
been a fine one, good work in sound old
timber, before the bits of the girder had
driven it into the wall; and the green pram
must have been the dowry of no ordinary
doll, but one with the best yellow curls,
whose blue eyes could move. One blue
columbine close by mourned alone for the
garden.

The wall and the vine and the bed and
the girder lay in an orchard, and some of
the apple-trees were standing yet, though
the orchard had been terribly worked by
shell fire. All that still stood were dead.
Some stood upon the very edge of craters;
their leaves and twigs and bark had been
stripped by one blast in a moment; and
they had tottered, with stunted, black,
gesticulating branches; and so they stood
to-day.

The curls of a mattress lay on the ground,
clipped once from a horse's mane.

After looking for some while across the
orchard one suddenly noticed that the

Cathedral had stood on the other side. It was draped, when we saw it closer, as with a huge grey cloak, the lead of its roof having come down and covered it.

Near the house of that petted doll (as I came to think of it) a road ran by on the other side of the railway. Great shells had dropped along it with terrible regularity. You could imagine Death striding down it with exact five-yard paces, on his own day, claiming his own. As I stood on the road something whispered behind me, and I saw, stirring round with the wind, in one of those footsteps of Death, a double page of a book open at Chapter two: and Chapter two was headed with the proverb: *"Un malheur ne vient jamais seul."* Misfortunes never come singly! And on that dreadful road, with shell-holes every five yards as far as the eye could see, and flat beyond it the whole city in ruin. What harmless girl or old man had been reading that dreadful prophecy when the Germans came down upon Albert and involved it, and themselves, and that book, all except those two pages, in such multiplication of ruin?

Surely indeed there is a third side to war: for what had the doll done, that used to have a green pram, to deserve to share thus in the fall and punishment of an Emperor?

A GARDEN OF ARRAS

VII

A GARDEN OF ARRAS

AS I walked through Arras from the
Spanish gate gardens flashed as I
went, one by one, through the houses.

I stepped in over the window-sill of one
of the houses, attracted by the gleam of a
garden dimly beyond: and went through
the empty house, empty of people, empty of
furniture, empty of plaster, and entered
the garden through an empty doorway.

When I came near it seemed less like a
garden. At first it had almost seemed to
beckon to passers-by in the street; so rare
are gardens now in this part of France, that
it seemed to have more than garden's
share of mystery, all in the silence there
at the back of the silent house; but when
one entered it some of the mystery went,
and seemed to hide in a further part of the

garden amongst wild shrubs and innumerable weeds.

British aeroplanes frequently roared over,
disturbing the congregation of Arras Cathedral a few hundred yards away, who rose
cawing and wheeled over the garden; for
only jackdaws come to Arras Cathedral
now, besides a few pigeons.

Unkempt beside me a bamboo flourished
wildly, having no need of man. On the
other side of the small wild track that had
been the garden path the skeletons of hot-
houses stood, surrounded by nettles; their
pipes lie all about, shattered and riddled
through.

Branches of rose break up through the
myriad nettles, but only to be seized and
choked by columbine. A late moth looks
for flowers not quite in vain. It hovers on
wing-beats that are invisibly swift by its
lonely autumn flower, then darts away over
the desolation which is no desolation to a
moth : man has destroyed man ; nature
comes back ; it is well : that must be the

brief philosophy of myriads of tiny things whose way of life one seldom considered before; now that man's cities are down, now that ruin and misery confront us whatever way we turn, one notices more the small things that are left.

One of the greenhouses is almost all gone, a tumbled mass that might be a piece of Babylon, if archeologists should come to study it.   But it is too sad to study, too untidy to have any interest, and, alas, too common : there are hundreds of miles of this.

The other greenhouse, a sad, ungainly skeleton, is possessed by grass and weeds. On the raised centre many flowerpots were neatly arranged once : they stand in orderly lines, but each separate one is broken : none contain flowers any more, but only grass. And the grass of the greenhouse lies there in showers, all grey. No one has tidied anything up there for years.

A meadowsweet had come into that greenhouse and dwelt there in that abode of fine tropical flowers; and one night an

elder tree had entered and is now as high
as the house; and at the end of the greenhouse grass has come in like a wave; for
change and disaster are far-reaching and
are only mirrored here. This desolate
garden and its ruined house are a part of
hundreds of thousands such, or millions.
Mathematics will give you no picture of
what France has suffered. If I tell you
what one garden is like, one village, one
house, one cathedral, after the German
war has swept by, and if you read my words,
I may help you perhaps to imagine more
easily what France has suffered than if
I spoke of millions. I speak of one garden
in Arras; and you might walk from there,
south by east for weeks, and find no garden
that has suffered less.

It is all weeds and elders. An apple-
tree rises out of a mass of nettles, but it is
quite dead. Wild rose trees show here
and there, or roses that have run wild like
the cats of No Man's Land. And once I
saw a rosebush that had been planted in

a pot, and still grew there as though it still remembered man, but the flowerpot was shattered like all the pots in that garden and the rose grew wild as any in any hedge.

The ivy alone grows on over a mighty wall, and seems to care not. The ivy alone seems not to mourn, but to have added the last four years to its growth as though they were ordinary years. That corner of the wall alone whispers not of disaster, it only seems to tell of the passing of years, which makes the ivy strong, and for which in peace as in war there is no care. All the rest speaks of war, of war that comes to gardens, without banners or trumpets or splendour, and roots up everything, and turns round and smashes the house, and leaves it all desolate, and forgets and goes away. And when the histories of the war are written, attacks and counter-attacks and the doom of Emperors, who will remember that garden?

Saddest of all, as it seemed to me watching the garden paths, were the spiders' webs

that had been spun across them, so grey
and stout and strong, fastened from weed
to weed, with the spider in their midst
sitting in obvious ownership. You knew
then as you looked at those webs across all
the paths in the garden that any whom you
might fancy walking the small paths still,
were but grey ghosts gone from thence, no
more than dreams, hopes and imaginings,
something altogether weaker than spiders'
webs.

And the old wall of the garden that
divides it from its neighbour, of solid stone
and brick, over fifteen feet high, it is that
mighty old wall that held the romance of
the garden. I do not tell the tale of that
garden of Arras, for that is conjecture and
I only tell what I saw, in order that some
one perhaps in some far country may know
what happened in thousands and thousands
of gardens because an Emperor sighed, and
longed for the splendour of war. The tale
is but conjecture, yet all the romance is
there; for picture a wall over fifteen feet

high built as they built long ago, standing
for all those ages between two gardens.
For would not the temptation arise to
peer over the wall if a young man heard,
perhaps songs, one evening on the other side?
And at first he would have some pretext
and afterwards none at all, and the pretext
would vary wonderfully little with the
generations, while the ivy went on growing
thicker and thicker. The thought might
come of climbing the wall altogether and
down the other side, and it might seem too
daring and be utterly put away. And then
one day, some wonderful summer evening,
the West all red and a new moon in the
sky, far voices heard clearly and white
mists rising, one wonderful summer day,
back would come that thought to climb
the great old wall and go down the other
side. Why not go in next door from the
street, you might say. That would be
different, that would be calling; that
would mean ceremony, black hats, and
awkward new gloves, constrained talk and

little scope for romance. It would all be
the fault of the wall.

With what diffidence, as the generations
passed, would each first peep over the wall
be undertaken. In some years it would
be scaled from one side, in some ages from
another. What a barrier that old red wall
would have seemed! How new the ad-
venture would have seemed in each age
to those that dared it, and how old to the
wall! And in all those years the elders
never made a door, but kept that huge and
haughty separation. And the ivy quietly
grew greener. And then one day a shell
came from the East, and, in a moment,
without plan or diffidence or pretext,
tumbled away some yards of the proud old
wall, and the two gardens were divided no
longer: but there was no one to walk in
them any more.

Wistfully round the edge of the huge
breach in the wall, a Michaelmas daisy
peered into the garden, in whose ruined
paths I stood.

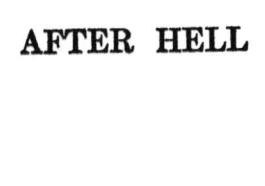

AFTER HELL

VIII

AFTER HELL

HE heard an English voice shouting "Paiper! Paiper!" No mere spelling of the word will give the intonation. It was the voice of English towns he heard again. The very voice of London in the morning. It seemed like magic, or like some wonderfully vivid dream.

He was only a hundred miles or so from England; it was not very long since he had been there; yet what he heard seemed like an enchanted dream, because only the day before he had been in the trenches.

They had been twelve days in the trenches and had marched out at evening. They had marched five miles and were among tin huts in quite a different world. Through the doorways of the huts green grass could be seen and the sun was shining on it. It was morning. Everything was strangely different. You saw more faces smiling. Men were not so calm as they had been during the last twelve days, the last six especially: some one was kicking a football at somebody else's hut and there was excitement about it.

Guns were still firing: but they thought of death now as one who walked on the other side of the hills, no longer as a neighbour, as one who might drop in at any moment, and sometimes did, while they were taking tea. It was not that they had been afraid of him, but the strain of expectancy was over; and that strain being suddenly gone in a single night, they all had a need, whether they knew it or not, of something to take its place, so the football loomed very large.

It was morning and he had slept long. The guns that grew active at dawn had not waked him; in those twelve days they had grown too familiar, but he woke wide

when he heard the young English soldier
with a bundle of three-days'-old papers
under his arm calling "Paiper, Paiper!" —
bringing to that strange camp the voice of
the English towns. He woke wide at that
wonder; and saw the sun shining cheerily,
on desolation with a tinge of green in it,
which even by itself rejoiced him on that
morning after those twelve days amongst
mud, looking at mud, surrounded by mud,
protected by mud, sharing with mud the
liability to be suddenly blown high and to
come down in a shower on other men's
helmets and coats.

He wondered if Dante when he came up
from Hell heard any one calling amongst
the verdure, in sunlight, any familiar call
such as merchants use, some trivial song
or cry of his native city.

A HAPPY VALLEY

IX

A HAPPY VALLEY

"THE enemy attacked the Happy Valley." I read these words in a paper at the time of the taking of Albert, for the second time, by our troops. And the words brought back Albert to me like a spell, Albert at the end of the mighty Bapaume-Albert road, that pathway of Mars down which he had stalked so tremendously through his garden, the wide waste battle fields of the Somme. The words brought back Albert at the end of that road in the sunset, and the cathedral seen against the West, and the gilded Virgin half cast down but incapable of losing dignity, and evening coming down over the marshes. They brought it back like a spell. Like two spells rather, that

some magician had mixed. Picture some
magician of old in his sombre wonderful
chamber wishing dreams to transport him
far off to delectable valleys. He sits
him down and writes out a spell on parch-
ment, slowly and with effort of aged memory, though he remembered it easily once.
The shadows of crocodiles and antique gods
flicker on walls and ceiling from a gusty
flame as he writes; and in the end he
writes the spell out wrongly, and mixes
up with the valleys where he would rest
dark bits of the region of Hell. So one
sees Albert again and its Happy Valley.

I do not know which the Happy Valley
is, for so many little valleys run in and out
about Albert; and with a little effort of
imagination, having only seen them full
of the ruin of war, one can fancy any of
them being once named happy. Yet one
there is away to the east of Albert which
even up to last Autumn seemed able to
bear this name, so secluded it was in that
awful garden of Mars; a tiny valley running

into the wood of Bécourt. A few yards higher up and all was desolation, a little further along a lonely road and you saw Albert mourning over irreparable vistas of ruin and wasted fields; but the little valley ran into the wood of Bécourt and sheltered there, and there you saw scarcely any signs of war. It might almost have been an English valley by the side of an English wood. The soil was the same brown clay that you see in the South of England above the downs and the chalk; the wood was a hazel wood such as grow in England, thinned a good deal, as English hazels are, but with several tall trees still growing; and plants were there and late flowers such as grow in Surrey and Kent. And at the end of the valley, just in the shadow of that familiar homely wood, a hundred British officers rest forever.

As the world is to-day perhaps that obscure spot, as fittingly as any, might be named the Happy Valley.

IN BETHUNE

X

IN BETHUNE

UNDER all ruins is history, as every tourist knows. Indeed the dust that gathers above the ruin of cities may be said to be the cover of the most wonderful of the picture-books of Time, those secret books into which we sometimes peep. We turn no more perhaps than the corner of a single page in our prying, but we catch a glimpse there of things so gorgeous, in the book that we are not meant to see, that it is worth while to travel to far countries, whoever can, to see one of those books, and where the edges are turned up a little to catch sight of those strange winged bulls and mysterious kings and lion-headed gods that were not meant for us. And out of the glimpse one catches from odd corners

of those volumes of Time, where old centuries hide, one builds up part by guesses,
part by fancy, mixed with but little knowl-
edge, a tale or theory of how men and
women lived in unknown ages in the faith
of forgotten gods.

Such a people lived in Timgad, and left
it probably about the time that waning
Rome began to call home her outposts.
Long after the citizens left the city stood
on that high plateau in Africa teaching
shepherd Arabs what Rome had been:
even to-day its great arches and parts of
its temples stand: its paved streets are
still grooved clearly with the wheel-ruts
of chariots, and beaten down on each side
of the centre by the pairs of horses that
drew them two thousand years ago. When
all the clatter had died away Timgad stood
there in silence.

At Pompeii city and citizens ended together. Pompeii did not mourn among
strangers, a city without a people, but was
buried at once, closed like an ancient book.

I doubt if any one knows why its gods
deserted Luxor, or Luxor lost faith in its
gods, or in itself; conquest from over the
desert or down the Nile, I suppose, or
corruption within. Who knows? But one
day I saw a woman come out from the back
of her house and empty a basket full of
dust and rubbish right into the temple at
Luxor, where a dark green god is seated,
three times the size of a man, buried as
high as his waist. I suppose that what I
saw had been happening off and on pretty
well every morning for the last four thousand years. Safe under the dust that that
woman threw, and the women that lived
before her, Time hid his secrets.

And then I have seen the edges of stones
in deserts that might or might not have
been cities: they had fallen so long that
you could hardly say.

At all these cities whether disaster met
them, and ruin came suddenly on to
crowded streets; or whether they passed
slowly out of fashion, and grew quieter

year by year while the jackals drew nearer
and nearer; at all these cities one can
look with interest and not be saddened
by the faintest sorrow for anything that
happened to such a different people so
very long ago.   Ram-headed gods, although their horns be broken and all their
worshippers gone; armies whose elephants
have turned against them; kings whose
ancestors have eclipsed their faces in heaven
and left them helpless against the onslaught
of the stars; not a tear is given for one of
these to-day.

But when in ruins as complete as Pompeii,
as desolate as Timgad amongst its African
hills, you see the remnant of a pack of
cards lying with what remains of the stock
of a draper's shop; and the front part of
the shop and the snug room at the back
gape side by side together in equal misery,
as though there had never been a barrier
between the counter with its wares and
the good mahogany table with its decanters;
then in the rustling of papers that blow

with dust along long-desolate floors one
hears the whisper of Disaster, saying "See;
I have come." For under plaster shaken
down by calamity, and red dust that once
was bricks, it is our own age that is lying;
and the little things that lie about the
floors are relics of the twentieth century.

Therefore in the streets of Bethune the
wistful appeal that is in all things lost far
off and utterly passed away cries out with
an insistence that is never felt in the older
fallen cities. No doubt to future times
the age that lies under plaster in Bethune,
with thin, bare laths standing over it, will
appear an age of glory; and yet to thousands that went one day from its streets
leaving all manner of small things behind,
it may well have been an age full of far
other promises, no less golden to them, no
less magical even, though too little to stir
the pen of History, busy with batteries
and imperial dooms. So that to these,
whatever others may write, the twentieth
century will not be the age of strategy but

will only seem to have been those fourteen
lost quiet summers whose fruits lie under
the plaster.

That layer of plaster and brick-dust lies
on the age that has gone, as final, as fatal,
as the layer of flints that covers the top
of the chalk and marks the end of an epoch
and some unknown geologic catastrophe.

It is only by the little things in Bethune,
lying where they were left, that one can
trace at all what kind of house each was,
or guess at the people who dwelt in it.   It
is only by a potato growing where pave-
ment was, and flowering vigorously under
a vacant window, that one can guess that
the battered house beside it was once a
fruiterer's shop, whence the potato rolled
away when man fell on evil days, and found
the street no longer harsh and unfriendly,
but soft and fertile like the primal waste,
and took root and throve there as its fore-
bears throve before it in another Continent
before the coming of man.

Across the street, in the dust of a stricken

house, the implements of his trade show
where a carpenter lived when disaster came
so suddenly, quite good tools, some still
upon shelves, some amongst broken things
that lie all over the floor. And further
along the street in which these things are
some one has put up a great iron shutter
that was to protect his shop. It has a
graceful border of painted irises all the
way up each side. It might have been
a jeweller that would have made such a
shutter. The shutter alone remains standing straight upright, and the whole shop is
gone.

And just here the shaken street ends
and all the streets end together. The rest
is a mound of white stones, and pieces of
bricks with low, leaning walls surrounding
it, and the halves of hollow houses; and
eyeing it round a corner, one old tower of
the cathedral, as though still gazing over
its congregation of houses, a ruined, melancholy watcher. Over the bricks lie tracks,
but no more streets. It is about the middle

of the town. A hawk goes over; calling
as though he flew over the waste, and as
though the waste were his. The breeze
that carries him opens old shutters and
flaps them to again. Old, useless hinges
moan; wall-paper whispers. Three French
soldiers trying to find their homes walk
over the bricks and groundsel.

It is the Abomination of Desolation, not
seen by prophecy far off in some fabulous
future, nor remembered from terrible ages
by the aid of papyrus and stone, but fallen
on our own century, on the homes of folk
like ourselves: common things that we
knew are become the relics of bygone days.
It is our own time that has ended in blood
and broken bricks.

IN AN OLD DRAWING-ROOM

XI

IN AN OLD DRAWING-ROOM

THERE was one house with a roof on it in Peronne. And there an officer came by moonlight on his way back from leave. He was looking for his battalion, which had moved, and was now somewhere in the desolation out in front of Peronne, or else was marching there, no one quite knew. Some one said he had seen it marching through Tincourt; the R. T. O. said Brie. Those who did not know were always ready to help, they made suggestions and even pulled out maps. Why should they not? They were giving away no secret, because they did not know, and so they followed a soldier's natural inclination to give all the help they could to another soldier. Therefore they offered their suggestions like old friends. They had never met before, might never meet again; but La France introduces you, and five minutes' acquaintance in a place like Peronne, where things may change so profoundly in one night, and where all is so tense by the strange background of ruin that little portions of time seem very valuable, five minutes there seems quite a long time. And so they are, for what may not happen in five minutes any day now in France? Five minutes may be a page of History, a chapter even, perhaps a volume. Little children with inky fingers years hence may sit for a whole hour trying to learn and remember just what happened during five minutes in France some time about now. These are just reflections such as pass through the mind in the moonlight among vast ruins and are at once forgotten.

Those that knew where the battalion was that the wandering officer looked for were not many; these were reserved and

each spoke like one that has a murder on his
conscience, not freely and openly: for of
one thing no one speaks in France and that
is the exact position of a unit. One may
wave one's hand vaguely eastwards and
say "Over there", but to name a village
and the people that occupy it is to offend
against the silence that in these days broods
over France, the solemn hush befitting so
vast a tragedy.

And in the end it seemed better to that
officer to obey the R. T. O. and to go by
his train to Brie that left in the morning;
and, that question settled, there remained
only food and sleep.

Down in the basement of the big house
with a roof there was a kitchen, in fact
there was everything that a house should
have; and the more that one saw of simple
household things, tables, chairs, the fire in
the kitchen, pieces of carpet, floors, ceilings
and even windows, the more one wondered;
it did not seem natural in Peronne.

Picture to yourself a fine drawing-room

with high ornamental walls, and all the air
about it of dignity, peace and ease, that
were so recently gone; only just, as it
might have been, stepped through the
double doorway; skirts, as it were of ladies
only just trailed out of sight; and then
turn in fancy to that great town streaming
with moonlight and full of the mystery
that moonlight always brings, but without
the light of it; all black, dark as caverns
of earth where no light ever came, blacker
for the moonlight than if no moon were
there; sombre, mourning and accursed;
each house in the great streets sheltering
darkness amongst its windowless walls,
as though it nursed disaster, having no
other children left, and would not let the
moon peer in on its grief or see the mon-
strous orphan that it fondled.

In the old drawing-room with twenty
others the wandering officer lay down to
sleep on the floor, and thought of old wars
that came to the cities of France a long
while ago. To just such houses as this,

he thought, men must have come before
and gone on next day to fight in other
centuries; it seemed to him that it must
have been more romantic then. Who
knows?

He had a bit of carpet to lie on. A few
more officers came in in the early part of
the night, and talked a little, and lay down.
A few candles were stuck on tables here and
there. Midnight would have struck from
the towers had any clock been left to strike
in Peronne. Still talk went on in low
voices here and there. The candles burned
low and were fewer. Big shadows floated
along those old high walls. Then the talk
ceased and every one was still: nothing
stirred but the shadows. An officer mut-
tered in sleep of things far thence and was
silent. Far away shells thumped faintly.
The shadows, left to themselves, went
round and round the room, searching in
every corner for something that was lost.
Over walls and ceiling they went and could
not find it. The last candle was failing.

It flared and guttered. The shadows raced over the room from corner to corner. Lost, and they could not find it. They hurried desperately in those last few moments. Great shadows searching for some little thing. In the smallest nook they sought for it. Then the last candle died. As the flame went up with the smoke from the fallen wick all the great shadows turned and mournfully trailed away.

THE HOMES OF ARRAS

XII

THE HOMES OF ARRAS

A S you come to Arras by the western road, by the red ramparts and the Spanish gate, Arras looks like a king. With such a dignity as clings to the ancient gateway so might a king be crowned; with such a sweep of dull red as the old ramparts show, so might he be robed; but a dead king with crowned skull. For the ways of Arras are empty but for brown soldiers, and her houses are bare as bones.

Arras sleeps profoundly, roofless, window-less, carpetless; Arras sleeps as a skeleton sleeps, with all the dignity of former days about it, but the life that stirs in its streets is not the old city's life, the old city is murdered.

I came to Arras and went down a street,

and saw back gardens glinting through the bare ribs of the houses. Garden after garden shone, so far as it could, though it was in October and after four years of war; but what was left of those gardens shining there in the sun was like sad faces trying to smile after many disasters.

I came to a great wall that no shell had breached. A cascade of scarlet creeper poured over it as though on the other side some serene garden grew, where no disaster came, tended by girls who had never heard of war, walking untrodden paths. It was not so. But one's fancy, weary of ruin, readily turns to such scenes wherever facts are hidden, though but by a tottering wall, led by a few bright leaves or the glimpse of a flower.

But not for any fancy of mine must you picture ruin any more as something graced with splendour, or as it were an argosy reaching the shores of our day laden with grandeur and dignity out of antiquity. Ruin to-day is not covered with ivy, and

has no curious architecture or strange
secrets of history, and is not beautiful or
romantic at all. It has no tale to tell of
old civilizations, not otherwise known, told
of by few grey stones. Ruin to-day is
destruction and sorrow and debt and loss,
come down untidily upon modern homes
and cutting off ordinary generations, smash-
ing the implements of familiar trades and
making common avocations obsolete. It
is no longer the guardian and the chronicle
of ages that we should otherwise forget :
ruin to-day is an age heaped up in rubble
round us before it has ceased to be still
green in our memory. Quite ordinary
wardrobes in unseemly attitudes gape out
from bedrooms whose front walls are gone,
in houses whose most inner design shows
unconcealed to the cold gaze of the street.
The rooms have neither mystery nor adorn-
ment. Burst mattresses loll down from
bedraggled beds. No one has come to
tidy them up for years. And roofs have
slanted down as low as the first floor.

I saw a green door ajar in an upper room :
the whole of the front wall of the house
was gone : the door partly opened so oddly
on to a little staircase, whose steps one could
just see, that one wondered whither it
went. The door seemed to beckon and
beckon to some lost room, but if one could
ever have got there, up through that
shattered house, and if the steps of that
little staircase would bear, so that one
came to the room that is hidden away at
the top, yet there could only be silence and
spiders there, and broken plaster and the
dust of calamity : it is only to memories
that the green door beckons; nothing
remains.

And some day they may come to Arras
to see the romance of war, to see where the
shells struck and to pick up pieces of iron.
It is not this that is romantic, not Mars
but poor, limping Peace. It is what is left
that appeals to you, with pathos and infinite charm, little desolate gardens that
no one has tended for years, wall-paper left

in forlorn rooms when all else is scattered, old toys buried in rubbish, old steps untrodden on inaccessible landings: it is what is left that appeals to you, what remains of old peaceful things. The great guns throb on, all round is the panoply of war, if panoply be the right word for this vast disaster that is known to Arras as innumerable separate sorrows, but it is not to this great event that the sympathy turns in Arras, nor to its thunder and show, nor the trappings of it, guns, lorries, and fragments of shells: it is to the voiceless, deserted inanimate things, so greatly wronged, that all the heart goes out: floors fallen in festoons, windows that seem to be wailing, roofs as though crazed with grief and then petrified in their craziness; railings, lampposts, sticks, all hit, nothing spared by that frenzied iron: the very earth clawed and torn: it is what is left that appeals to you.

As I went from Arras I passed by a grey, gaunt shape, the ghost of a railway station standing in the wilderness haunting a waste

of weeds, and mourning, as it seemed, over
rusted railway lines lying idle and purpose-
less as though leading nowhere, as though
all roads had ceased, and all lands were
deserted, and all travellers dead : sorrowful
and lonely that ghostly shape stood dumb
in the desolation among houses whose doors
were shut and their windows broken. And
in all that stricken assembly no voice spoke,
but the sound of iron tapping on broken
things, which was dumb awhile when the
wind dropped. The wind rose and it
tapped again.

www.ingramcontent.com/pod-product-compliance
Lightning Source LLC
Chambersburg PA
CBHW050830180626
46814CB00004B/1555